Cambridge Discovery Education™
INTERACTIVE READERS

Series editor: Bob Hastings

WILD AUSTRALIA!

Simon Beaver

CAMBRIDGE UNIVERSITY PRESS
Cambridge, New York, Melbourne, Madrid, Cape Town,
Singapore, São Paulo, Delhi, Mexico City

Cambridge University Press
32 Avenue of the Americas, New York, NY 10013-2473, USA

www.cambridge.org
Information on this title: www.cambridge.org/9781107621657

© Cambridge University Press 2014

This publication is in copyright. Subject to statutory exception and to the provisions of relevant collective licensing agreements, no reproduction of any part may take place without the written permission of Cambridge University Press.

First published 2014

Printed in Hong Kong, China, by Golden Cup Printing Company Limited

A catalog record for this publication is available from the British Library.

Library of Congress Cataloging-in-Publication Data

Beaver, Simon.
 Wild Australia! / Simon Beaver.
  pages cm. -- (Cambridge discovery interactive readers)
 978-1-107-62165-7 (pbk. : alk. paper)
 1. Australia, Ancient--Juvenile literature. 2. English language--Textbooks for foreign speakers. 3. Readers (Elementary) I. Title.

DU96.B44 2014
994--dc23

2013013700

ISBN 978-1-107-62165-7

Additional resources for this publication at www.cambridge.org

Cambridge University Press has no responsibility for the persistence or accuracy of URLs for external or third-party Internet Web sites referred to in this publication and does not guarantee that any content on such Web sites is, or will remain, accurate or appropriate.

Layout services, art direction, book design, and photo research: Q2ABillSMITH GROUP
Editorial services: Hyphen S.A.
Audio production: CityVox, New York
Video production: Q2ABillSMITH GROUP

Contents

Before You Read: Get Ready! 4

CHAPTER 1
Australia and Its Wildlife 6

CHAPTER 2
Mammals 8

CHAPTER 3
Birds 12

CHAPTER 4
Reptiles 14

CHAPTER 5
River and Sea Life 16

CHAPTER 6
What Do You Think? 20

After You Read 22

Answer Key 24

Glossary

Before You Read:
Get Ready!

There are many exciting animals in Australia. You are going to read about some of them.

Words to Know

Complete the sentences with the correct words.

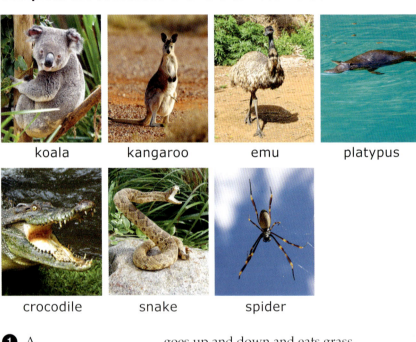

koala   kangaroo   emu   platypus

crocodile   snake   spider

1. A _____ goes up and down and eats grass.
2. A _____ has eight legs.
3. A _____ has big teeth and eats meat.
4. A _____ is a swimming animal with brown hair.
5. A _____ has a long body and no legs.
6. A _____ is gray and lives in trees.
7. An _____ is a big bird that cannot fly.

Words to Know

Complete the sentences with the correct words.

wildlife   dangerous   islands   forest

tunnel   venomous   sea

1. The _____ is very big. It's all salt water.
2. Some animals are pets, but animals that live in nature are called _____.
3. Hawaii is a group of _____.
4. Don't play games in the road! It's _____!
5. A _____ is a place with a lot of trees.
6. Don't go near snakes and spiders in Australia. Some are _____.
7. The road goes through the _____.

CHAPTER 1

Australia and Its Wildlife

A LONG TIME AGO, AUSTRALIA WAS PART OF A SUPERCONTINENT CALLED GONDWANA.

Because Australia left the supercontinent[1] 130 million years ago, the animals here are different from animals in other places.

[1]**supercontinent:** millions of years ago, a very big island with the continents Antarctica, South America, Africa, and others all together as one

Video Quest

Unique Australia

Watch the video about Australian wildlife. What problems do some animals have? What answers do they find to those problems?

The **wildlife** can be **dangerous** to people: there are venomous snakes and spiders, and crocodiles, too.

Some animals only come from Australia, like the koala and the platypus. There are also many beautiful birds. Some are big and cannot fly, like the emu. The Australian animal that everybody knows is the kangaroo. Its babies live in a pouch[2] on the mother's body.

You can find exciting animals all over Australia.

[2] **pouch:** like a bag; the kangaroo has one in its body

CHAPTER 2

Mammals

MAMMALS ARE ANIMALS THAT START THEIR LIVES AS BABIES AND NOT AS EGGS. THEY DRINK THEIR MOTHER'S MILK. MANY MAMMALS IN THE WORLD ONLY COME FROM AUSTRALIA.

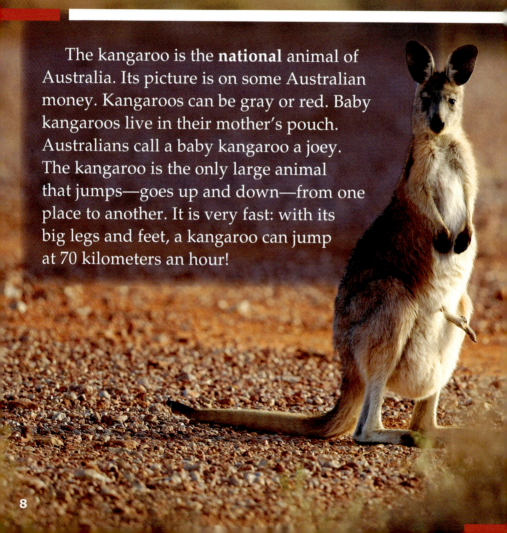

The kangaroo is the **national** animal of Australia. Its picture is on some Australian money. Kangaroos can be gray or red. Baby kangaroos live in their mother's pouch. Australians call a baby kangaroo a joey. The kangaroo is the only large animal that jumps—goes up and down—from one place to another. It is very fast: with its big legs and feet, a kangaroo can jump at 70 kilometers an hour!

The koala is a very beautiful animal with gray hair and a black nose. It lives in the trees, and it finds its food there. It has a pouch for its babies, like the kangaroo. Koalas sleep for most of the day because the weather in Australia can be very hot. Some people say the Aborigine word *koala* means "does not drink," but this is wrong. It's only a name. The koala gets a lot of water from the plants it eats, but like every animal it also drinks water when it's **thirsty**.

EVALUATE

Why do you think Australia has a kangaroo on some of its money?

The Tasmanian devil lives in Tasmania, the second, smaller **island** of Australia. It has a pouch, too. It eats other animals. It has a big head and black fur.[3] It also has long hairs on its face. It uses the hairs to feel things, like cats do. The hairs tell the animal what is near it. When the first people came to Tasmania, they ate many Tasmanian devils. There are not many Tasmanian devils living in Australia today.

[3] **fur:** hair on the bodies of animals like cats

The dingo is a dog, but it is not a pet! We think the first dingoes came to Australia with people many thousands of years ago. Dingoes eat meat, and farmers do not like them because they eat sheep. Dingoes can be dangerous. If you visit a place where there are dingoes, you must watch your children. In 1980, a mother in Australia lost her baby. She said a dingo took it. People thought that she wasn't right, but she was!

Video Quest

Koalas

Watch the video about a beautiful Australian mammal. Where does it live? Why does it need a tunnel? Write down your answers.

CHAPTER 3
Birds

AUSTRALIA HAS A LOT OF DIFFERENT BIRDS. FOR MILLIONS OF YEARS, UNTIL PEOPLE CAME TO AUSTRALIA WITH DOGS AND CATS, THERE WERE NO OTHER ANIMALS TO EAT THE BIRDS. SO MANY KINDS OF BIRDS DIDN'T NEED TO FLY.

The emu is Australia's biggest and most famous bird. It cannot fly, but it can run very fast: 50 kilometers an hour! Emus can be taller than a man. Most of them live in forests, and they eat plants. There are now emu farms in Australia, because people like to eat their meat.

Emu eggs are very big. An Aborigine story says that when the world was young, somebody sent an emu egg into the sky and made the sun. Aborigines also see a big picture of a black emu in the night sky.

Another famous Australian bird is the kookaburra. There are different kinds of kookaburra with different colors. When you listen to them, they sound like[4] people laughing. Kookaburras eat snakes and other birds. Sometimes when people are cooking outside their homes, kookaburras fly down and take the food.

[4]**sound like:** seem like something, from what you see or hear

CHAPTER 4

Reptiles

SNAKES, CROCODILES, AND LIZARDS ARE REPTILES. THEY ARE ANIMALS THAT COME FROM EGGS.

Most snakes in Australia are dangerous. You can die if they put their venom in your body. One of the most venomous snakes in the world is the Inland Taipan. It lives in hot places and eats small animals. It's difficult to see because its color changes. This snake isn't **usually** a problem, because it doesn't like to be near people.

Crocodiles live in **oceans** or rivers. They have big teeth and long bodies. They can be six meters long. They live for a long time: some live for more than a hundred years!

A lizard

Crocodiles eat meat, fish, and sometimes people! It isn't good to go near a crocodile. But it isn't always easy to see crocodiles. You can sometimes think they are a part of a tree in the water.

Video Quest

Skinks

Watch the video about an interesting lizard in Australia called the blue-tongued skink. Why does it have a blue tongue?[5] Is it a dangerous animal?

[5] **tongue:** the pink thing in your mouth that you use to speak and eat

15

CHAPTER 5

River and Sea Life

THERE IS A LOT OF LIFE IN AUSTRALIA'S RIVERS AND SEAS.

The platypus lives in Australia's rivers. It's a mammal, but it's very different from other mammals. It's the only mammal to come from an egg, and it's venomous, too!

People in England first saw the platypus in 1798. They didn't think it was one animal. They thought it was two animals together. The platypus sleeps for 14 hours a day and eats small animals. It uses **electricity** to "see" these animals! No other mammal does this.

The Great Barrier Reef is a wall of coral[6] in the **sea** near Australia. It's 600,000 years old, and it's very big – 2,600 kilometers long! Very small sea animals make coral and live in it. **Coral reefs** are a great home for animals and plants. The Great Barrier Reef is home to 1,500 kinds of fish and more than 2,000 kinds of plants. Some of them cannot live in any other place, so they need the reef.

[6]**coral:** hard bodies made by some small sea animals; they can be in many colors and look like rocks

The sea is warmer now than it was many years ago. This is bad for coral, and so it's bad for the animals on coral reefs, too. Another problem for coral is an interesting kind of **starfish**. It eats the animals that make coral. There are sometimes too many of these starfish. In 2000, they ate 66 percent[7] of coral animals on a lot of reefs!

---
[7] **percent:** for or out of every 100

A starfish

The dugong is sometimes called the "sea cow." It's the only mammal that always lives in the sea and eats only plants. Most dugongs live near Australia. They can live a long time – up to 73 years! Dugongs like to be together, but often they cannot stay together. They eat a lot, so sometimes they must leave the others to find food.

A long time ago, when people first saw a dugong in the sea, they thought it was a person. They went home and told stories of an animal that was half-woman and half-fish – a mermaid.

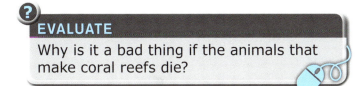

EVALUATE
Why is it a bad thing if the animals that make coral reefs die?

CHAPTER 6

What Do You Think?

GOVERNMENTS GET MONEY FROM THE PEOPLE IN THEIR COUNTRY. THEY OFTEN USE SOME OF THIS MONEY TO HELP THE ANIMALS IN THEIR COUNTRY.

The government[8] in Australia made a road in a place where koalas live and travel. This was bad for the koalas. The koalas needed to go easily and safely from one place to another for food. The government decided to pay money to make a tunnel under the road for the koalas to use.

[8]**government:** a group of people who tell all the people in their country what they must do and cannot do

Another country that did this is India. Tigers[9] are in danger, so the Indian government uses money to pay for big parks where tigers can live safely. There are now about 40 of these parks in the country.

Do you think it is OK for governments to use people's money to pay for things like this? Is it a good idea for governments to help animals? Why or why not?

Does your government pay to help animals? Which animals? Does it help the animals where you live?

[9] **tiger:** a big, dangerous cat that has yellow and black fur

After You Read

True or False

Read the sentences and choose Ⓐ (True) or Ⓑ (False). If the book does not tell you, choose Ⓒ (Doesn't say).

1 A joey is a baby skink.
- Ⓐ True
- Ⓑ False
- Ⓒ Doesn't say

2 Emus can only walk slowly.
- Ⓐ True
- Ⓑ False
- Ⓒ Doesn't say

3 There is an Aborigine story about the emu.
- Ⓐ True
- Ⓑ False
- Ⓒ Doesn't say

4 Koalas do not drink water.
- Ⓐ True
- Ⓑ False
- Ⓒ Doesn't say

5 Kookaburras eat other birds, but they don't eat snakes.
- Ⓐ True
- Ⓑ False
- Ⓒ Doesn't say

6 Crocodiles can live for more than a hundred years.
- Ⓐ True
- Ⓑ False
- Ⓒ Doesn't say

7 The Great Barrier Reef is the home of more than 2,000 kinds of fish.
- (A) True
- (B) False
- (C) Doesn't say

8 The dugong has its picture on some Australian money.
- (A) True
- (B) False
- (C) Doesn't say

Complete the Chart

Write the names of five animals that you want to see in Australia in the first column below. What kind of animal are they: fish, bird, mammal, or reptile? Why do you want to see them?

Animal	Kind of animal	Why I would like to see it

Answer Key

Words to Know, page 4
❶ kangaroo ❷ spider ❸ crocodile ❹ platypus ❺ snake
❻ koala ❼ emu

Words to Know, page 5
❶ sea ❷ wildlife ❸ islands ❹ dangerous ❺ forest
❻ venomous ❼ tunnel

Video Quest, page 7
Kangaroo: hard to find grass and water. It jumps from place to place because it uses less energy than walking.
Koala: must live in hot weather. It sleeps a lot because the weather is hot.
Snakes, spiders, and platypuses: animals try to eat them. They are venomous, so animals won't eat them.

Evaluate, page 9
Answers will vary.

Video Quest, page 11
The koala lives in trees. It needs a tunnel because people put a road in its home.

Video Quest, page 15
To make animals think it's dangerous, but it's not.

Evaluate, page 19
Thousands of other animals can only live near this coral. If the coral dies, these animals may die, too.

True or False, page 22
❶ B ❷ B ❸ A ❹ B ❺ B ❻ A ❼ B ❽ C

Complete the Chart, page 23
Answers will vary.